For the young of all ages, everywhere
—DEMI

Henry Holt and Company, Inc.

Publishers since 1866

115 West 18th Street

New York, New York 10011

Henry Holt is a registered
trademark of Henry Holt and Company, Inc.

Copyright © 1997 by Demi
All rights reserved.

Published in Canada by Fitzhenry & Whiteside Ltd.,
195 Allstate Parkway, Markham, Ontario L3R 4T8.

Library of Congress Cataloging-in-Publication Data
Demi.
Buddha stories / Demi.
Summary: A collection of ten tales from Buddha.
I. Jataka stories, English.   [1. Jataka stories.]   I. Title.
BQ1462.E5D46   1997   294.3'823—dc20   96-31253

ISBN 0-8050-4886-3
First Edition—1997
Typography by Martha Rago
The artist used traditional Chinese inks with pen and brush
on vellum to create the illustrations for this book.
Printed in the United States of America on acid-free paper. ∞
1   3   5   7   9   10   8   6   4   2

BUDDHA STORIES

by DEMI

Henry Holt and Company

New York

THE ART

The world's first printed book was a Buddhist *sutra*, or teaching, made with woodblocks in 600 A.D. It contains one picture and text in gold on deep indigo rice paper, in scroll form. *Buddha Stories* is modeled on that first book. The fine lines were created using pen and ink—and sometimes a single mouse whisker.

JATAKAS

Buddhists believe that the Buddha was reborn many times on Earth, sometimes as a king, sometimes as a peasant, sometimes as an animal such as an elephant or lion, or a bird, fish, reptile, or insect. In each of these lives, it is believed, Buddha found a way to help others.

The *Jatakas* are the Buddha's stories, celebrating the power of compassion, love, wisdom, and kindness. Buddha told these stories, about 550 of which have survived until the present, to his disciples 2,500 years ago. They were first written down by hand in Ceylon in Singhalese, then translated into Pali about 430 A.D. Since then, they have been translated into many different languages around the world.

All my life I have collected Jataka stories in many languages, but I think the most basic source in English is *The Jataka* translated from the Pali by various hands (London: Pali Text Society, 1895).

And while the Buddha sat, and all those around him listened, these are the stories he told. . . .

THE LION KING

Once upon a time, a rabbit went to sleep under a coconut tree. When he woke up, a big coconut fell on the ground and exploded with a *bang!* At the sound, the rabbit jumped up and cried, "The earth is breaking up! The earth is breaking up!" He ran off as fast as he could, crying, "The earth is breaking up!"

Soon another rabbit joined him, then another, until there were one hundred rabbits running and crying, "The earth is breaking up!"

A frightened deer heard their cries and joined in the flight, followed by a boar, an elk, a buffalo, an ox, a rhinoceros, a tiger, and an elephant. A lion king heard their cries and thought, The earth is *not* breaking up. There is some mistake. And if I don't do something, they will all run into the river and drown!

He ran in front of them and roared, "*Stop!* Who says the earth is breaking up?"

The boar said, "The rabbits said."

The buffalo said, "The elk said."

The rhinoceros said, "The ox said."

The elephant said, "The tiger said the earth was breaking up!"

All nodded and pointed to the first rabbit.

"Is it true the earth is breaking up?" asked the lion king.

"Yes, O great lion, it is!" said the rabbit. "I woke up from my nap and heard the sound of the earth breaking up!"

"Then," said the lion king, "you and I will go back to the place where the earth began to break up and see for ourselves if it's true!"

With the rabbit holding on to his back, the lion king ran off as fast as the wind to the coconut tree. When the lion king saw the broken coconut he said to the rabbit, "You silly rabbit! The sound of a coconut breaking up does not mean that the earth is breaking up!"

And they ran back to the other animals to explain the mistake.

When one person tells a falsehood, one hundred repeat it as true.

THE TURTLE AND THE GEESE

A turtle lived in a pond at the foot of a hill. Two wild geese looking for food saw the turtle, and the turtle began talking with them. The next day the geese came again and the turtle talked with them again, and soon all three were great friends.

"Turtle friend," Mr. Goose said one day, "we have a beautiful home far away. We are going to fly there tomorrow. It will be a long but worthwhile journey. Do you want to come with us?"

"How could I? I have no wings!" said the turtle.

"We could take you if you promise to keep your mouth shut and not say a word to anybody!"

"I can do that!" said the turtle. "Take me with you!"

The next day the geese brought a stick and each held one end of it. "Now," said Mr. Goose, "grip the middle of the stick with your mouth and don't say a word to anybody until we reach home!" The geese then sprang into the air with the turtle between them, holding fast to the stick.

Children below saw the two geese flying with the turtle and cried out, "Look at the turtle up in the air! Did you ever see anything so silly in your whole life?" And the children broke into peals of laughter. The turtle's pride was deeply wounded, and he opened his mouth to say, "If I am carried on a stick, what business is it of yours?" But when he let go of the stick, he fell to his death.

Disaster can come from opening your mouth at the wrong time.

THE BLACK BULL

On a rich farm in India, a beautiful black calf was born. He was so perfectly formed and so strong that his master named him Beauty. He fed him the finest rice and treated him with kindness. In time, Beauty grew into a giant bull of the most amazing strength. He thought to himself, I should do something to repay my master's kindness.

He said to his master, "O kind master! Why don't you have a contest for a thousand gold pieces to see which bull can pull a hundred carts loaded with stones?"

His master thought the idea excellent and arranged a great race. As the race began, he jumped on Beauty's back and fiercely whipped his sides. Then he shouted, "Pull, you demon! Pull!" But Beauty had never heard such words or felt his master's whip before. The bull would not budge an inch. His master lost the contest and went home in defeat. He went to bed even though the sun was shining. Beauty strolled over to his window and looked in.

He asked, "Master, why are you taking a nap?"

"Taking a nap? I've lost so much money I'll never sleep again!"

Beauty asked, "Master, in all my life, have I ever hurt you or your children?"

"Never," said his master.

"Then why were you so cruel to me? Did the thought of so much money make you forget all respect for your friend and servant?"

His master was silent.

Beauty said, "Arrange another contest, this time for two thousand gold pieces, but remember to treat me kindly."

So his master arranged another contest. This time, he stroked Beauty's back and said softly, "Beautiful bull, please show us your amazing strength!" And Beauty gave a single pull and moved so far ahead of all the other bulls that he beat them by many miles.

Treat others with kindness and your deeds will be rewarded.

THE BEAUTIFUL PARROTS

Once upon a time, two parrots lived in a deep green forest. Both were gorgeous, with red, yellow, and blue feathers, but one was wise and the other was foolish. A hunter trapped the two birds and gave them to the king as a present. The king was pleased with his beautiful birds and put them in a golden cage with golden dishes full of honey, parched corn, and sugar water to drink. The king talked and played with the parrots, and soon they became the favorites of the whole court.

Then one day a hunter trapped a big black monkey and gave it to the king as a present. Soon, all the attention was paid to the monkey. He made funny faces and became the favorite. The wise parrot said nothing. But the foolish parrot complained, "Now the monkey gets the attention that belongs to us!"

The wise parrot said, "By what right does all the attention belong to us?"

The foolish parrot replied, "Because we were go good! So loyal and true! And we never bit anyone or squawked! We were such well-behaved birds!"

The wise parrot said,

> "Attention belongs to nobody:
> Gain and loss and praise and blame
> Pleasure, pain, dishonor, fame
> All come and go like a breeze,
> Why should a little parrot grieve?"

Meanwhile, as time went on, the monkey did not seem so funny anymore. Soon he began to scare the children. The king became angry and ordered the monkey back into the forest. Once again the parrots were the favorites of the whole court and the foolish parrot sang with joy.

But the wise parrot warned,

> "Gain and loss and praise and blame
> Pleasure, pain, dishonor, fame
> Come and go like the spring,
> Why should a little parrot sing?"

Riches and fame come and go like the wind.

THE CUNNING WOLF

Once upon a time, a wolf lived on a rock by the banks of the Ganges River. Suddenly, rising winter floods surrounded his rock and he was marooned. The wolf sat on his rock with no food to eat and no way of getting any.

As I must sit here with nothing to do until the floodwaters subside, thought the wolf, I might as well think about the meaning of life: I have not always been the best of wolves. I have been frightening, greedy, hungry, and fierce. I am going to become a new wolf. I am going to become religious!

And so, folding his paws in front of him as holy men do, he sat on his rock and thought he must look very holy. Pleased with himself, he adjusted his tail and said, "Now I'll begin my holy fast. I will eat nothing till the waters subside!" But Buddha decided to test the wolf. Buddha could change himself into any shape he wished, and he became a plump little goat jumping about on the rock. The wolf took one look at the little goat and began to drool.

"Forget about starving today—I'll starve tomorrow!" he said, and sprang at the goat. But the goat got away. The wolf sprang again. But the goat got away again. The wolf jumped, leaped, and chased the goat until he was breathless, whereupon he gave up, exhausted.

Suddenly, he cheered up, thinking, At least I have not broken my fast! I am a new wolf after all!

Then the goat vanished and Buddha appeared in its place. He said to the wolf with some scorn, "You did promise to reform, but your promise you didn't keep. Words that are hardest to live by are easiest to speak!"

It is easier to make a promise than to keep it.

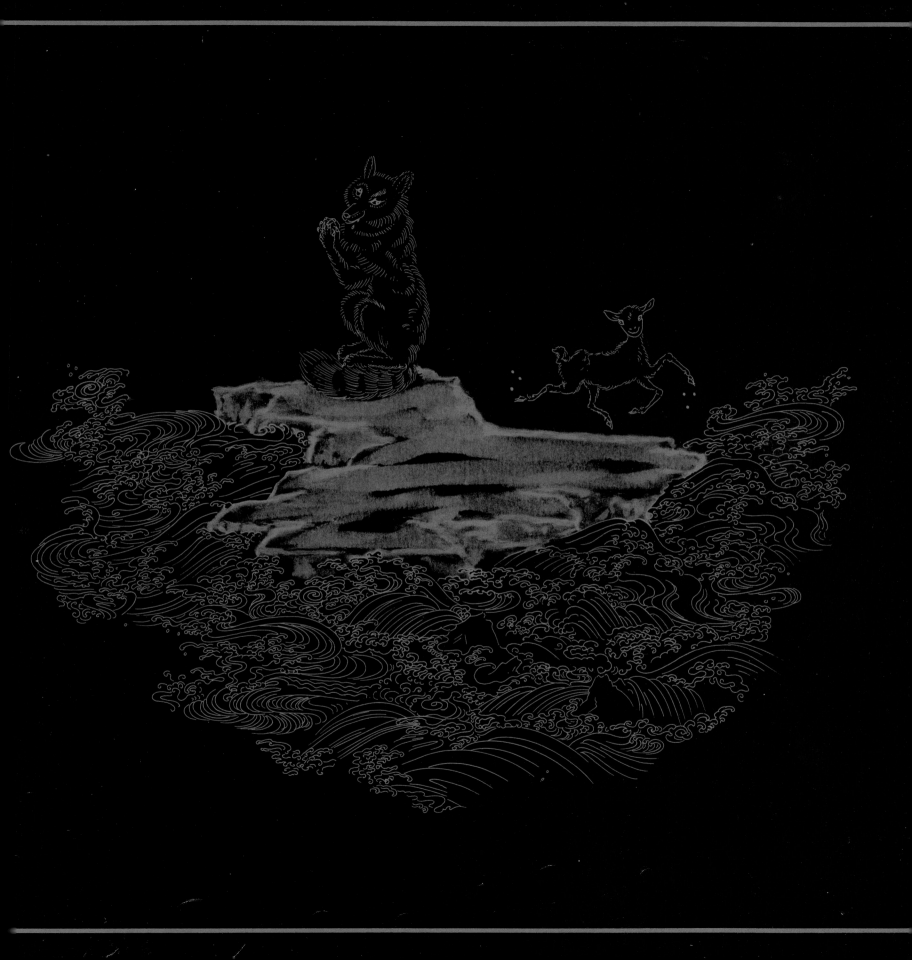

THE LITTLE GRAY DONKEY

Once upon a time, there was a merchant who carried his goods on the back of a donkey. At the end of each day he would look for some rich fields of barley and rice. Then, when no one was looking, he would throw a lion skin over the donkey, turn him loose, and let him eat to his heart's content. When farmers saw this creature in the twilight, they thought he was a lion and didn't dare come near him! The merchant became cocky. He thought, I sell to the people by day, and I rob them by night. I am so tricky! I am so smart!

One sunny day, as the merchant was having breakfast, he let his donkey loose in a rich barley field with the lion skin on. These farmers are so stupid, they won't know the difference between day and night, he thought.

The farmers did think it was the lion again, but this time they summoned all the other villagers, who descended on the field waving hoes and rakes and beating drums and gongs. The donkey was scared out of his wits! He gasped and brayed, "Hee-haw! Hee-haw! Hee-haw! Hee-haw!" and the lion skin fell off his back. When the farmers saw it was only a donkey, they roared with laughter. They chased him away with hoes and rakes and beating drums. And they chased his master away, as well.

Don't be deceived by a donkey in a lion's skin.

THE CLEVER CRAB

One summer long ago, a fish pond was rapidly drying up from lack of rain. A crane on the bank said to the fish, "I know of a pond deep in the woods where there is plenty of water. I could carry you there, one by one."

"No crane ever wants to help a fish!" said the king of fish.

"If you don't believe me," said the crane, "I'll take you there and bring you back, and you can tell all the other fish about it yourself."

The king of fish figured he would just as soon be eaten by the crane as dry up in his pond, so he accepted the offer. The fish held on to the crane's back with his fins, and they flew deep into the woods. There the king of fish saw a great pond—cool and shady, pure and sparkling.

"Wonderful!" said the king of fish. "Now take me back so I can tell the other fish about it!"

So back they went. All the fish wanted to go to the great pond, and the crane picked them up one fish at a time and carried them away—not to the great pond, but to a cave where he ate them one by one. Soon he had eaten all the fish. There was only a crab left in the little pond.

"Crab," said the crane, "I'll take you to the great pond as I did all the fish."

"OK," said the crab. "But you must let me hold on to your neck with my claws."

The crane knew about the tight grip of crabs, but he was so hungry, he agreed.

So the crab held on to the crane's neck with his claws, and they flew into the cave.

"OK. Let go of my neck," said the crane.

The crab looked around and said, "I see no great pond. All I see is a great pile of fish bones!"

"Yes!" said the crane. "And soon your shell will be all that's left of you!"

But the crab tightened his grip so sharply that the crane's head fell off.

"Not my shell, but your bones will be left to dry in remorse!" said the crab, crawling away. After a few days, he found the great pond deep in the woods—cool and shady, pure and sparkling—and lived there happily ever after.

If you cheat on the earth, the earth will cheat on you.

THE MONKEY KING

Once upon a time, there was a monkey king who ruled over eighty thousand monkeys. In his kingdom was a mango tree as big as the moon. The monkeys jumped all over the tree, eating the fruit and picking up those that fell to the ground. One of the tree's branches spread over a river, and sometimes a mango fell into it and floated downstream.

"Danger will come if a mango floats downstream!" predicted the monkey king, and he ordered the monkeys to catch any mangoes that fell into the water. But one night, unseen by the monkeys, a mango fell into the water and floated far downstream. In the morning, when a human king who lived in a river palace went to take his bath, he saw the huge, beautiful fruit. After tasting it, he had to have more, and he set out with his men to find the source upstream. In the evening, after a long, hard search, they spotted the enormous mango tree full of lovely ripe fruit. Since the men were tired, they camped beneath it for the night. When all the men had fallen asleep, the monkey king with his eighty thousand monkeys crept into the tree and, moving from branch to branch, started eating up the mangoes. But the human king heard the monkeys and woke up.

He called to his men, "Save the fruit! Save the fruit!"

His men surrounded the tree and aimed their arrows at the monkeys. The monkeys trembled with fear but the monkey king said, "Do not be afraid! I will save you!"

Quickly he wound his tail around the branch of the tree that spread over the river, then leaped across the river and caught a branch of a banyan tree on the other side, making a bridge of his own back! Then he called to the monkeys, "Come, monkeys! Run out onto the branch, across my back, and down the banyan tree!"

The monkeys did as their king told them to. They were all safe and sound.

The human king, witnessing this scene, was amazed. He thought, All I am doing is saving fruit, while this monkey king has just saved his whole troop! I have learned a great lesson today. He went back to his kingdom, forgetting about the fruit, and began doing good works for all his people.

If the family lives in harmony, all affairs will prosper.

THE GOLDEN GOOSE

Once upon a time, there was a goose who had beautiful golden feathers. One day, flying in the heavens, the goose looked down and saw a very poor woman with two daughters all dressed in rags. The goose thought about the hard time they must be having and said to himself, If I gave them a golden feather, the mother could sell it at the marketplace and they would have enough to eat! So away the goose flew to the poor woman's house.

"What do you want?" said the poor woman angrily. "I have nothing to give you!"

"But I have something to give you!" said the goose, and he pulled out one of his golden feathers and gave it to her. Then away he flew. The woman grabbed the feather and her daughters and off they went to the marketplace, where they bought lots of good things to eat. From time to time the goose returned, and on each occasion he presented the woman with a golden feather, so that eventually they lived in comfort. But one day the woman thought, I do not trust this goose. He may fly away and never come back. Then we will be poor again. We must pull out all his feathers the next time he comes.

When she told her daughters, they cried, "No! No! That will hurt the goose! We will not pull out his feathers!"

But the woman was very greedy. The next time the goose returned, she grabbed him with both hands and pulled out all his feathers. She didn't know that the feathers of the golden goose were magic, and if pulled out against his will, they turned a dirty white, like soiled chicken feathers. And that is what happened. The woman could not believe her eyes. She cried in despair.

Her daughters were horrified to see goose feathers scattered around. They gently lifted up the poor plucked goose and went into the woods. There they cared for him until his feathers grew back, shiny and gold. To reward them for their kindness, the goose found them loving husbands. But because of her incurable greed, their mother lived worse off than before and new disasters greeted her every day.

The greatest wealth is the wealth of kindness.

THE MAGIC PIG

One day an old woman found two young pigs and brought them home with her in a basket. She named them Big Snout and Little Snout and treated them like her own children. In time they became big and fat. Many people thought they would be delicious and wanted to buy them to eat. But the old woman always said, "These are my children. How could I sell my own children?"

One festival day some ruffians were eating and drinking. They wanted more food and remembered the old woman's two fat pigs. They went off to get them. Banging drunkenly on her door, they offered her money, but she would not take it. Then they returned with weapons, ready to take the two pigs by force. Little Snout began to tremble all over and cried, "Today we are doomed!"

But Big Snout said, "Do not be afraid!" and he began reciting "The Perfection of Love," a great prayer that disperses all evil. Magically, his voice began to sound louder and louder and filled the old woman's house. It traveled outside, and the sound of love pierced the ears of the ruffians, who put down their weapons. The sound of love traveled into the palace, where it reached the king's ears. He asked, "Who is making this lovely sound?"

He followed it back to the old woman's home, where he was amazed to find that the source of the sound was a pig. He honored the old woman with a grand palace where she and both pigs lived—clothed, perfumed, and jeweled. Five hundred royal guards protected them at all times. On holy days Big Snout preached "The Perfection of Love," and peace, truth, and love reigned throughout the kingdom.

Heaven remembers those whose hearts are true.

THE MAGIC ELEPHANT

Once a dazzling white elephant was born, and because of his great beauty, he became the elephant of the king. Adorned on festival days, he would carry the king through the streets and everyone would say, "What a magnificent elephant!"

Since no one ever said anything flattering about the king, the king became jealous of the elephant and thought of a plan to get rid of him. The king summoned the elephant's trainer.

"This elephant is not well trained!" said the king.

"Indeed he is!" said the trainer.

"If he is, then he can climb to the top of the highest mountain!" said the king.

So the trainer mounted the dazzling white elephant and rode him up to the highest mountain's peak. The king and his courtiers followed in horse-drawn wagons.

"If he is so well trained," said the king, "he can stand on three legs at the edge of the mountaintop!" The trainer signaled and the elephant stood on three legs.

"Now make him stand on his two front legs!" yelled the king. The elephant raised his back legs and stood on his front legs.

"Now on his back legs!" roared the king. The obedient elephant raised his front legs and stood on his back legs.

"Now on one leg!" screamed the king. And the elephant stood on one leg.

"If he is so well trained," screeched the king, "make him stand on the air!"

Surely the king must want him to fall off the cliff, the trainer thought. So he whispered in the elephant's ear, "Great white elephant, the king wants you to fall off the cliff to your death. He is not worthy of you. If you have magic powers, rise up in the air and fly with me to the next kingdom!"

And the great white elephant rose straight up into the air!

The trainer then yelled down to the king, "This great white elephant is too good for a worthless fool like you; none but a wise and good king is worthy to be his master."

And off they flew to the next kingdom, whose wise king in time reduced the worthless king to ashes.

Pride leads to a fall, but humility is rewarded in the end.